Puffin Books

HILD AT ALLOTMENT LANE SCHOOL

Miss Mee's class at Allotment Lane School has a new girl. She's called Hild. Hild is the kind of girl you just can't miss. She's got a loud voice and beautiful golden orange hair, and wherever she is, she's always the centre of attention.

Life is never dull with Hild around. She always manages to get what she wants, whether it's a share of someone else's lunch or her favourite school dinner. There's always something happening when Hild is there — such as a dramatic rescue in the swimming baths, or a dinosaur visiting!

Everyone at Allotment Lane School loves Hild, and so will you after reading about all her funny adventures.

Other books by Margaret Joy

ALLOTMENT LANE SCHOOL AGAIN
HAIRY AND SLUG
THE LITTLE LIGHTHOUSE KEEPER
SEE YOU AT THE MATCH
TALES FROM ALLOTMENT LANE SCHOOL

HILD AT ALLOTMENT LANE SCHOOL

Margaret Joy

illustrated by
Joyce MacDonald

PUFFIN BOOKS

PUFFIN BOOKS

Published by the Penguin Group
27 Wrights Lane, London w8 5TZ, England
Viking Penguin Inc., 40 West 23rd Street, New York, New York 10010, USA
Penguin Books Australia Ltd, Ringwood, Victoria, Australia
Penguin Books Canada Ltd, 2801 John Street, Markham, Ontario, Canada L3R 1B4
Penguin Books (NZ) Ltd, 182–190 Wairau Road, Auckland 10, New Zealand

Penguin Books Ltd, Registered Offices: Harmondsworth, Middlesex, England

First published by Faber and Faber Limited 1987
Published in Puffin Books 1989
1 3 5 7 9 10 8 6 4 2

Copyright © Margaret Joy, 1987
Illustrations copyright © Joyce MacDonald, 1987
All rights reserved

Made and printed in Great Britain by
Richard Clay Ltd, Bungay, Suffolk

for
my mother
and Norah

Monday Playtime

At the top of Allotment Lane stands a school for boys and girls aged five to eleven; it's probably very like your school. There are tall children, short children, dark children and fair children. There are children with brothers and sisters, and children with none. There are several boys called Jason and Gary, and several girls called Sarah and Tracy. But there is only one Hild.

Hild has been at the school only a few days, but already everyone knows her. Her real name is Hilda, but no one calls her that. It's much easier for the other children to shriek, 'Seen you, Hild!' when they're playing hide-and-seek, or for Miss Mee to sigh, 'Oh, Hild, not *again*,' when Hild somehow manages to spill a pool of

1

paint from an unspillable pot with the lid jammed on tight.

In the playground you can spot Hild easily, as she's always in the middle of a crowd, telling an exciting story or scowling at someone who has disagreed with her; she has a very loud voice, too, so everyone knows it's Hild. She isn't frightened of anyone, however big or tough they are – she'll argue with anyone, her fat freckled cheeks growing redder and redder, and her big green eyes flashing.

This playtime Hild was standing watching the others put on their coats to go out to play; most of them had something in their pockets to eat.

'What did your Mum give you?' asked Mary.

'My Mum's gone to stay with my Gran, 'cause she was fed up with having rows with my Dad,' said Hild. 'What've you got?'

Mary unfolded her greaseproof packet: first one end, then the other, then the two sides. Flat on the greaseproof paper lay two crisp cream crackers, sandwiched together with thick butter: they looked delicious. Hild's mouth watered. Her green eyes greedily watched Mary's white teeth take a small, neat bite: snap!

'Ooh, look,' said Hild.

'Can't see anything,' said Mary, blowing crumbs everywhere.

'There,' said Hild. 'Worms.'

'Where?' squeaked Mary.

Hild pointed to the bottom of the cream cracker sandwich.

'Look,' she said. 'Little yellow worms.'

'That's butter,' said Mary.

'Butter worms,' said Hild. 'Look, and there's some squiggling on top – see?'

Mary looked, horrified. Yes, butter had curled up out of the holes on top. She held it away from her, with a look of disgust on her face.

'Shall I take the squiggly worms away?' asked Hild politely.

'Eugh, yuk,' said Mary, handing over the cream cracker sandwich. Hild disappeared, stuffing buttery cream cracker

into her mouth as fast as she could.
Round a corner of the school wall, she
found Michael and Gary, dipping into the
bag of crisps Paul was holding out. Hild
looked again. The crisps were in a blue
packet – that meant they were salt- and
vinegar-flavoured, her favourite.

'You playing Superman?' she asked the
boys.

'In a minute,' said Gary. 'When we've
finished these crisps.'

'Can I have one?' asked Hild.

'They're just for us,' said Michael. 'We're Paul's friends.'

'I'm Paul's friend, too, aren't I, Paul?' asked Hild. 'Aren't I your friend, Paul? Go on – let me have some crisps: I'll let you be Superman.'

'OK,' said Paul. 'I'll be Superman.' He pushed the packet with the rest of the crisps into Hild's outstretched hands, and zoomed off across the playground. Gary and Michael turned to look at Hild, but she had already disappeared round the corner, cramming the rest of the crisps into her mouth as fast as she could.

When they were all gone, she put her hands in her pockets and walked slowly round the edge of the playground. Her big green eyes noticed everything. She stopped to watch Rosemary, Barbara and Nasreen. They were counting out the Smarties that Rosemary had tipped from a tube.

'One for you,' said Rosemary, putting it in Nasreen's lap.

'One for you,' she said, putting one in

her twin's lap.

Hild quietly sat down next to them.

'I just like the orange ones,' she said.

'Oh, all right,' said Rosemary. She put an orange one in Hild's lap. 'And one for me,' she said. Then she went round again: 'One for you, one for you, one for you, and one for me.'

By the time she had shared them all out, the bell was ringing for the end of playtime. Everyone lined up to go back into class.

'You all look very happy,' said Miss Mee. 'You must have had a good playtime.'

'I brought some crisps,' said Paul.

'I brought cream crackers,' said Mary.

'We brought Smarties,' said Rosemary and Barbara.

'I didn't bring anything,' said Hild, looking at Miss Mee sadly.

'Oh, poor Hild,' said Miss Mee. 'Never mind. There – you can have my biscuit. I didn't want it with my cup of tea.'

'Thanks,' said Hild, and gave Miss Mee

a sad little smile. She began to crunch the ginger biscuit noisily. Mary and Paul and Gary and Michael and Rosemary and Barbara and Nasreen all looked at one another – and then at Hild. She looked back at them with her big green eyes, and shook her head.

'I didn't bring anything at all,' she said, '– honest.'

Hild at the Baths

Hild has bright golden-orange hair, which is always cut by her father. He waits until it has grown down into straight wisps on to her shoulders, then one day he says, 'Time we tidied up that hair.' He gets her to stand on a piece of newspaper in the middle of the kitchen floor. He fetches the kitchen scissors – which are none too sharp, and sometimes still greasy from cutting the rind off the bacon – and starts to trim her fringe.

First he cuts at the right, then at the left, then a cut or two to try to even it up in the middle. After that, he cuts thick, jagged chunks from the sides and the back, trying to get her hair level all the way round. Lastly, he places his large thumb on the crown of Hild's head, and pushes

her round with the other hand. As she
slowly turns, her father tries to even up

the jagged lengths of hair with wild
swoops of the scissors. Then he stands
back, looks at the heaps of golden-orange

hair on the newspaper and says, 'You'll do, Hild, you'll do.'

Everyone at school knows when Hild has had a hair-cut, for she arrives next day looking like a plump little Easter chick, with a piece of jagged golden-orange shell perched on its head. But Hild's hair is always bright and shining, because she washes it in the bath with washing-up liquid every Saturday night; and the school nurse, who comes to look at the children's heads, always says that Hild's hair is a credit to her Dad.

One day when Hild's hair was nearly straggling on to her shoulders and ready for one of her Dad's trims, she came to school with her hair in bunches tied with ribbon. No one had ever seen Hild with bunches before. People gathered round to inspect her.

'Our Trudi did it,' said Hild: Trudi was her big sister.

'You've got ribbons in,' said Sue.

Hild nodded, beaming with pride.

'But they're *black*,' said Laura.

'Yeah, I got them off our Trudi,' said Hild. 'She'd finished with her brazzy, see, so she cut the straps off and tied them on my bunches.'

'No one wears black ribbons to school,' said Brenda.

'Yes, they do,' snapped Hild. '*I* do.'

A few days later it was Class 1's turn to go to the Baths. They clambered up the high steps of the coach, clutching their swimming things and chattering at the tops of their voices.

'Bagsy sit at the back!' shouted Hild, panting with the effort of pushing past the others who were before her in the queue. She raced to the back of the coach and sat bouncing in the middle of the back seat. From here she had the best view of the rest of the coach. Also, as Miss Mee always sat at the front, Hild felt free to bounce up and down on the springy seat, or even to turn round and kneel up to make gruesome faces at drivers in the traffic behind.

'You always get the best seat, you do,'

grumbled Paul.

'Only 'cause I got here first,' said Hild.

'But you pushed,' said Imdad.

'Yes, I bet you gave me bruises when you shoved past me, Hild Hooson,' said Wendy. 'I'll have a look when I've got my cossie on.'

Hild took no notice of Wendy, but sat still with her plump little legs sticking straight out in front of her. She had her black ribbons in again, and her bunches stuck out sideways in golden-orange tufts, where Trudi had pulled them tight.

When they reached the Baths, the boys went into the Boys' Changing Room, while the girls followed Miss Mee to the Girls'. They quickly got ready to go in the water.

'Look there, Hild Hooson,' said Wendy, pulling her vest up to show her ribs. 'Look – see that mark there? – That's what your elbow did. It's a bruise, see: it's already turning brown.'

Hild peered at Wendy's skin.

'That's not a bruise,' she snorted.

'That's dirt!'

'How dare you say I'm dirty, Hild Hooson!' shouted Wendy, and went for Hild.

Miss Mee turned round just in time to pull them apart.

'Behave yourselves!' she said. 'Now, are you all ready? – Then let's show that nice baths attendant what a good class you are.'

They went down the corridor, splashed their way through the foot pool – and there was the Big Pool with the diving boards towering at one end. The blue water lay as still as glass; the Allotment Lane children were going to be the first in. Miss Mee helped them all on with inflatable cuffs to keep them afloat, then, shivering and excited, they let themselves down into the water at the shallow end.

Soon the air of the bath hall was full of echoing shrieks and shouts and splashing, as the children got used to the feel of the water. Miss Mee stood at one side, dressed in her pink and grey trainers and track-suit; at the other side sat the baths attendant in his white T-shirt and shorts, keeping an eye on everything that went on.

'Morning, Miss Mee,' he called across.

'Morning, Gareth,' she smiled back.

Hild's sharp ears had been listening. She rather liked Gareth; her big sister, Trudi, knew him. Trudi said he was dishy. Hild thought Gareth was dishy, too. He was taller than her Dad, and was really sun-tanned, and had a nice face. She knew his job was to dive in and rescue people who couldn't swim and got into difficulties. Miss Mee blew her whistle.

'Come to the side, Class 1,' she called – and the lesson began. They held on to the bar and practised kicking and leg movements. Then they held on to the bar with their feet and practised hand and arm movements. Then they let go and tried the arm and leg movements together – that was much harder, and lots of people only swam a little way, but one or two managed to splash along a few metres before sinking down and then bouncing to their feet, spluttering and laughing. After that, they tried floating on their backs. Hild was good at this; she even closed her eyes and enjoyed the feeling – it was like lying on a giant's hand. Miss Mee let them have the last five minutes playing; then she blew her whistle and it was time to get out.

'Aah,' said everyone. No one ever liked leaving the bath. Dripping and shivering, they pulled off their cuffs and dropped them into the basket Gareth kept them in.

'Back to the changing room now,' ordered Miss Mee.' But don't *run*, you'll slip over.'

A moment later there was a shout.

'My ribbon, my ribbon!'

Miss Mee turned round to see one of Hild's black ribbons floating gently on top of the water at the deep end. Hild was looking at the ribbon, then across at Gareth, who had jumped to his feet. Then – perhaps Hild's foot slipped as she ran to the edge of the bath – suddenly, with an echoing splash, she half fell, half slipped, into the deep end. The water bubbled over her head.

'Oh, Hild!' yelled Miss Mee.

Hild's golden-orange head shot to the surface again, streaming with water.

'Help, Gareth!' she spluttered, and did a furious doggy-paddle with her hands, then started to sink again.

Gareth knew what to do. He calmly lifted down from a hook on the wall a long pole with an enormous net on one end. He lowered the net down into the deep water and lifted it gently up . . . with Hild inside. She looked very surprised to be caught like a fish in a net and pulled to the side by Gareth. She looked quite disappointed, too, when it was Miss Mee who hauled her out of the net and stood her up on the edge of the bath.

'Oh, *Hild!*' said Miss Mee again, wrapping a towel round her and hurrying her back to the other girls in the Changing Room. For once Hild was quite quiet, and

let Miss Mee help her to dry quickly and
change back into her warm clothes. They
went back to the entrance hall, where
they met the boys.

'Just a minute, Miss
Mee,' called a voice
from the corridor.

Gareth came
hurrying up and
handed Hild a damp
black ribbon bow.
Hild's cheeks flushed
rosy; she grinned up at
Gareth and her green
eyes shone.

'You rescued me,
didn't you?' she
demanded.

'Well . . . sort of,'
smiled Gareth.

'Our Trudi thinks
you're dishy,' said
Hild. 'So do I.'

'Oh, er ... thanks,' said Gareth. 'You're not so bad yourself.'

As they sat in the coach on the way back to Allotment Lane, Sue asked:

'Did he really rescue you?'

'Yes, 'course he did – didn't you see him?'

'No, we were all back in the Changing Room,' said Sue.

'Ah, well, yes . . .' said Hild, with a faraway look in her eyes, 'Well, he saw me in the deep end, drowning, and he ran to the diving board, and climbed up to the very top one and dived right down with lots of somersaults – you know, like you see on telly – and landed next to me in the water without even a single splash, and put his hand under my chin and helped me swim back to the side.'

She thought for a moment, then added:

'And he said he'd never seen such nice black ribbons before – so there.'

A Bunch of Tulips

One spring morning Laura came into class with a large bunch of flowers wrapped carefully in a piece of tissue paper.

'They're out of our garden,' said Laura. 'To brighten up the classroom.'

'Oh, what lovely tulips,' said Miss Mee, showing everyone. 'They're beautiful, Laura.'

'I like the jazzy ones best,' said Laura. 'The yellow ones with red edges.'

'Mmm – I think the bright scarlet red ones are my favourites,' said Miss Mee. 'Would you like to look for a tall vase under the bench, Laura? Then if you half fill it with water, you can arrange the flowers and we'll put them where everyone can see them.'

Hild was standing watching and scowling. She had a horrible scowl which wrinkled up her forehead and half shut her green eyes – and made her look very cross. Miss Mee noticed Hild's horrible scowl.

'Cheer up, Hild, we'll be going in the Hall soon. It's our day for the big apparatus. You always enjoy that.'

'Great!' said everyone, starting to pull off their shoes and socks and undo buttons.

'We haven't got any flowers in our garden,' scowled Hild. 'Our dogs have dug it all up. My Dad says he's going to cover it over with concrete.'

'Never mind,' said Miss Mee. 'You can still enjoy our classroom flowers. Why don't you go and look at them, and then get ready for the big apparatus?'

'Don't want the big apparatus,' said Hild, scowling even more. 'Don't want to go in the Hall. Don't want to get undressed.'

'It's your favourite lesson, Hild,' said Miss Mee. 'You know you always come to school extra early on big apparatus days.'

'Not today I didn't,' scowled Hild. 'I didn't want to come today, but Dad made me. He was waiting for the washing machine man. He pushed me out and shut the door behind me.'

In the end, Miss Mee had to coax Hild and help her to undress, because Hild refused to do anything herself. At last everyone was sitting ready in vest and pants and with bare feet. They went quietly into the Hall and sat on one of the mats, ready for Miss Mee to tell them which group they were in. Children from the Top Class had put out all the apparatus ready for them: the climbing bars and the ropes, the big box and the mat to jump on to, the benches to balance along.

When everyone was sorted into groups, they started work – climbing, swinging, jumping, hanging and balancing – everyone, that is, except Hild. She kept one hand clutched to her waist, as she went to stand next to Miss Mee.

'Come on, Hild; come and show me how well you balance,' said Miss Mee. 'I'll hold your hand.'

Hild scowled and kept one hand at her waist, but let Miss Mee take hold of her other hand to help her walk up the plank. Then Hild stopped and looked down at her toes.

'Do you like my varnish, Miss Mee?' she asked. 'Trudi let me borrow hers and do my toe-nails. That colour's called scarlet.'

Hild's tiny toe-nails were a brilliant, shiny red.

'It's a lovely colour, my favourite,' said Miss Mee admiringly. 'Now I'll let go and see if you can walk along, balancing, to the end.'

Miss Mee let go and Hild held out both arms to balance herself – and then it happened: Hild yelled –

'M' 'lastic's snapped!' and snatched at her pants, which were slowly slipping down past her knees. She wobbled wildly on top of the balance, but Miss Mee grabbed her and lifted her down just in time. She whispered to Hild:

'You'd better go back to class and change; then come back in here.'

Hild went off, holding her pants up with one hand. The rest of the lesson was very peaceful. Hild came back and sat at the side and scowled at everyone because they were enjoying themselves, and she wasn't. After the lesson, when everyone was dressed again, when the last tie was tied and the last popper popped, the children went out to play. Hild stayed behind with Miss Mee.

'It's the washing machine,' she explained. 'It's broken down, so all my pants are waiting to be washed – except these old ones with the loose elastic.'

Miss Mee lifted down Class 1's box of spare clothes.

'There are some pants in here,' she said. 'You can borrow some.'

Hild dived down and pulled out a pair of pink pants decorated with white flowers and little bows.

'Ooh, Miss Mee – ooh, these are lovely – they're nicer than all of mine! Can I borrow these?'

Miss Mee said there were so many pairs in the box that Hild could keep the pink pair.

'For ever?' asked Hild.

'Yes, for ever,' said Miss Mee.

The next week on apparatus day, Hild came into school early. She had her hands behind her back and her green eyes were shining.

'Guess what, Miss Mee,' she said.

'What?' asked Miss Mee.

'It's big apparatus day, so I've got the pink pants on, so everyone can see them – and guess what else.'

'What else?' asked Miss Mee.

'I've got something for you.'

She pulled a bunch of red tulips from behind her back and slapped them down on Miss Mee's table.

'Oh, Hild, they're lovely!' said Miss Mee. 'My favourite scarlet tulips. Thank you very much!'

She thought for a moment, then she said:

'But I thought you didn't have any flowers in your garden, Hild?'

'I'll get a vase and put some water in it, shall I, Miss Mee?' asked Hild – but she hadn't answered Miss Mee's question.

Later on that morning, Mr Gill came into Class 1.

'Good morning, everyone,' he said. 'I've just had a phone call I want to tell you about. It was from the man in charge of the park behind the school. He said someone had been picking some of the flowers in the park. He asked if it was any of the children at Allotment Lane School – but I told him I was sure none of you would pick flowers from the park, because you would know that was stealing, wouldn't you?'

'Yes, Mr Gill,' said everyone.

'That's good,' he said, smiling at everyone, then going out again.

At playtime Miss Mee was on duty in the playground. She walked round holding her cup of coffee, watching everyone playing. Hild and Laura came running up to her.

'Can we take your cup back to the staffroom?' asked Hild.

'All right, when I've finished,' said Miss Mee. 'You can carry the cup, Hild, and Laura can knock on the staffroom door.'

'Did you like my tulips?' asked Hild.

'You know I did,' said Miss Mee. 'I think they're really beautiful. – But where did you get them?'

Laura giggled.

'*I* know,' she said. 'But it's a secret.'

She turned to Hild. 'Shall I tell her?' she asked.

'Oh, go on then,' said Hild.

'I let her pick some out of our garden,' said Laura. ' 'Cause she wanted to bring you a present, and we've got lots.'

'But I asked her first,' said Hild hastily '– I wouldn't just take them without asking, that would be stealing, wouldn't it?'

'Oh, yes, it would,' said Miss Mee. 'But how kind of Laura to let you share her tulips.'

'That's 'cause she's my friend,' said

Hild. 'Now – have you finished? Can we take your cup?'

A Walk and a Wish

One afternoon when the air was cold and the sky was blue and bright, Miss Mee said:

'This is just the day for a walk. Go and change into your outdoor things, and we'll go down the lane.'

She put her coat on and took some plastic carrier bags from the cupboard.

'They're for specimens,' she said. 'Interesting things we might find.'

They crossed the playground and set off down the lane, kicking through piles of leaves and exclaiming at all the things they saw.

'Ooh, look, there's an empty bird's nest in the middle of the hedge,' said little Larry. 'But there's all thorns and things in the way.'

Miss Mee lent him one of her old gloves. He put it on and pushed his arm into the hedge right up to his shoulder, then carefully pulled the nest out. It was made of grass and lined with moss and tiny feathers.

'There's an old bedstead dumped in that field,' said Stevie, peering through a hole in the hedge. 'And an old mattress with all the stuffing coming out.'

'The birds might use that for their nests,' suggested Michael.

They started to put specimens into the carrier bags: different kinds of red berries, all sorts of coloured leaves, one or two toadstools, some long grasses and some lumpy pieces of wood with interesting shapes. Then they stood and watched three little birds that seemed to be playing hide-and-seek in the bushes. After that they crossed the field and went into a little wood behind the allotments.

It was very quiet. They stood still and looked up to where the branches of the trees criss-crossed to make a kind of roof.

The wood was shady and rather gloomy. There was a sudden cracking of twigs and a flapping of wings as a large pigeon flew up from a branch. Everyone stared at it, startled. Jean shivered and whispered:

'I don't think I like it in here.'

'Wolves live in woods, don't they, Miss Mee?' asked Hild. '– Like the one in Red Riding Hood, and they hide behind trees and say –'

'BOO!' shouted Michael, and everyone shrieked.

Jean clung to Miss Mee's arm.

'I think we should sing,' said Ian.

'All right,' said Miss Mee. 'How about our autumn song? – you know – the one that sounds like "London Bridge".'

They began to sing, first with little trembly sounds, then with their loudest voices, which echoed through the wood.

'When the leaves are turning brown, turning
brown, turning brown,
When the leaves are turning brown, then we
know it's autumn.

*When the leaves are falling down, falling
      down, falling down,
When the leaves are falling down, then we
      know it's autumn.'*

'That's better,' said Jean. She let go of
Miss Mee and began to kick up the piles
of leaves so they rustled and crackled.

Then everyone else joined in and soon felt
better again. A little wind began to whis-
per through the branches; a few more
leaves slowly fell to the ground.

'My Grandma says you can wish if you
catch a falling leaf,' said Wendy. 'But you
mustn't tell anyone what you wish for, or
it won't come true.'

After hearing that, everyone wanted to

catch a falling leaf, but it was harder than it looked; at the last moment a little puff of wind seemed to blow the leaves as they fell, so that they twisted out of the children's outstretched hands and floated to the ground.

'Time to go,' called Miss Mee, and they began to race after her, out of the wood and into the sunshine again. Hild wasn't listening. Up above her head she could see a large golden leaf spiralling slowly down towards her. She held her breath as the leaf fell nearer and nearer.

'Gotyer!' said Hild. She crinkled the leaf between her hands, shut her eyes tightly, and made a wish.

At dinner-time the next day Hild ate everything as usual, then held up her hand for a second helping.

'My goodness, Hild,' said Mrs Doran, the dinner lady, 'I don't know where you put it all – have you got hollow legs to fill up?'

'It's my bestest dinner today,' said Hild. She went round the edge of the plate with her spoon to scoop up the last drops of gravy.

'Your favourite, is it?' said Mrs Doran. 'Steak and kidney pie? I'll tell Cook; she'll be pleased you enjoyed it so much – And there's ginger pudding and custard next.'

'Oooh, great,' said Hild, licking her spoon clean.

After dinner Hild helped to put the chairs away. Mrs Eccles, the cook, leant through the hatch and called to Hild:

'Did you enjoy your dinner today, then?'

'Yes, it was all my bestest – steak and kidney pie, then ginger pudding and custard,' said Hild.

She went on stacking chairs, thinking hard. Then she said:

'We went to the woods yesterday with Miss Mee. I caught a leaf and made a wish.'

'Oh, yes?' said Mrs Eccles. 'What did you wish for, then?'

'Oh . . . er . . . something nice for my birthday,' said Hild.

'When's your birthday, then?' asked Mrs Eccles.

'Oh . . . um . . . next Friday,' said Hild.

Mrs Eccles went back into the kitchen and told Mrs Doran what Hild had been saying.

'Poor little thing,' said Mrs Doran. 'Do you know she eats every scrap that's put in front of her? I don't expect her Dad gets round to making pies and puddings.'

'It'd be nice if we could make Hild's birthday a bit special for her, wouldn't it?' said Mrs Eccles thoughtfully. 'We could always have her favourite dinner again, I suppose, she'd like that.'

So on Friday it was steak and kidney

pie for dinner again, followed by ginger pudding and custard. Hild put her hand up as usual for second helpings, and Mrs Doran saw that she had a good full plate every time.

'It's because you're the birthday girl today, Hild,' she whispered.

Mrs Eccles stood at the hatch and watched, smiling to see Hild enjoying it so much. Miss Mee took her own empty plate back to the kitchen.

'That was delicious, Mrs Eccles,' she said.

'Well, it's no bother doing the same meal again in one week,' said Mrs Eccles.

'It's worth it to give her a birthday treat, poor little thing.'

She explained to Miss Mee about Hild's wish.

'Oh, I didn't know it was her birthday today,' said Miss Mee.

So when it was time for afternoon play, Miss Mee gave Hild a chocolate biscuit wrapped in silver paper, for another little birthday treat. At hometime, Hild's Dad came to meet her. He had his two dogs with him on long pieces of string. Hild bent down to make a fuss of them.

'Hild's been working hard today, Mr Hooson,' said Miss Mee. 'And then it was her favourite dinner – Cook made it specially, as a birthday treat.'

'Oh, yes?' said Hild's Dad. 'Birthday treat, eh? Bit early, isn't it?'

Hild looked up at Miss Mee and her Dad. Her green eyes gleamed, but she didn't say anything.

'Early, Mr Hooson?' said Miss Mee, puzzled.

'Yes – her birthday's not till after Christmas. It's another three months till your birthday, isn't it, Hild?' he said.

He tugged at the strings and walked off with Hild and the dogs. Miss Mee went straight back into the classroom and looked in the register – yes, it was true: today wasn't Hild's birthday at all.

'Oh, the little madam!' exclaimed Miss Mee. 'The little baggage! Fancy telling Cook that today was her birthday.'

Next day Miss Mee said to Hild:

'You told Cook a great big fib about your birthday, didn't you, Hild?'

'It was just a sort of mix-up,' said Hild. 'But I *did* make a wish when I caught that leaf, honest I did.'

'What did you *really* wish for then?' asked Miss Mee.

'Can't tell you that, can I, Miss Mee?' said Hild '– Or it won't come true.'

Harvest Festival

The bell rang and another day began at Allotment Lane School. Children streamed inside from the playground. Many of them were carrying bunches of flowers, bulging paper bags or plastic carriers. The next day was to be the school's Harvest Festival. Class 1 children put what they had brought on a side table in the classroom.

'Here's three tins of beans,' said Laura.

'I've got some mangoes,' said Imdad. 'What's in your bag?'

'Lots of plums off our tree,' said Brenda.

'Mine's special, isn't it, Miss Mee?' boasted Paul. 'It's from our shop.'

He staggered across to the side table and set down the large basket he was

39

carrying. Everyone gathered round to inspect it – a flat basket, big as a tray, beautifully filled with fruit. There was a hand of yellow bananas, a bunch of purple grapes, some shining red apples, two golden pears, some fluffy peaches, and several little bright orange tangerines – all nestling together on a bed of soft green tissue, covered over with cling-film and tied with a bow of bright green ribbon.

Just then Hild burst in, clutching a large carrot – it was almost the same colour as her hair.

'Sorry I'm late, Miss Mee,' she gasped. 'I had to go down the doctor's with our Dad, because his hands were all scratched and bleeding, because the rabbit got loose and the cat chased the rabbit, and when Dad picked up the rabbit, the cat went for Dad, and –'

'Oh, your poor old Dad,' said Miss Mee sympathetically. 'Is he all right now?'

'Oh, yes, he's gone home again now. He said you could have this for the Harvest Festival –' She gave Miss Mee the carrot. 'There's plenty left for the rabbit.'

'Thank you, Hild,' said Miss Mee. 'Put it over here with the other things.'

'Who brung that?' demanded Hild, staring at the basket of fruit.

'That's from Paul's greengrocer's shop,' said Miss Mee. 'Isn't it beautiful?'

Hild said nothing, but went on staring at the basket with its pretty bow of green satin ribbon. At hometime, Miss Mee said:

'Don't forget that it's our Harvest Festival tomorrow, and we'll be showing your Mums and Dads our Great Big Enormous Turnip play! Then afterwards, we'll share out all the fruit and flowers and vegetables, so that each of you has a little present to give to an elderly person who lives near you. If you know someone who's old, or poor, or not very well, we'll see that you take them a share of all these lovely things.'

The next day was very busy. Lots of the parents and little brothers and sisters came and sat in the Hall, which was

bright with vases of flowers, bowls of fruit, stacks of tinned food and heaps of vegetables. Right in the front lay a large, shiny brown loaf, in the shape of a sheaf of wheat.

Hild kept turning round and stretching this way and that.

'I can't see my Dad,' she said to Ian – but then Mr Gill came in and people stopped talking. Mrs Owthwaite began to play the piano. Some of the Big Boys and Girls picked up their instruments: recorders, tambourines and drums. Everyone joined in singing:

All things bright and beautiful,
All creatures great and small,

42

All things wise and wonderful,
The Lord God made them all.

Some of the older children read out some poems and sang more songs. Mr Gill stood up and said how lovely the Hall looked, and how all the food was going to be sent home with the children to be given to old people who were unwell or housebound.

'What's housebound?' whispered Hild to Ian.

'Stuck at home,' said Ian.

'Now it's the moment we've all been waiting for,' said Mr Gill. 'Class 1 are going to act out their favourite story, The Great Big Enormous Turnip.'

Michael was the little old man; he pulled on his wellies and planted turnip seed in his garden. Lots of the children curled up small – they were the seeds. The sun shone and the wind blew and the rain fell, and the seeds started to grow into big fat turnips. The little old man pulled up all the turnips easily, except for one: a great big enormous turnip. That was Hild – and she *wouldn't* let Michael pull her out of the ground.

He had to call the little old woman – that was Nasreen – to help. Then they had to call the boy – that was Stevie, then the girl – that was Brenda, then Asif the dog, and Rosemary the cat, and last of all, little Larry, who was the tiny mouse. They all pulled and pulled and pulled and PULLED. With a tremendous shout, the great big enormous Hild-turnip came shooting out of the ground and fell on top of Michael, Nasreen, Stevie, Brenda, Asif, Rosemary and little Larry.

Everyone who was watching laughed and clapped. Hild beamed and scrambled to her feet again. She waved wildly at her big sister, Trudi, sitting at the back of the Hall.

Later on, when they were back in their own classroom, the children helped Miss Mee to share out the fruit, flowers and vegetables, so that they each had a bag of good things to take with them.

'We'd better have a raffle for Paul's basket of fruit,' said Miss Mee. 'Here's a piece of paper for everyone. Write your name on it and fold it up.'

They dropped the papers into an empty tin. Miss Mee stirred them round and Paul picked one out. He unfolded it and showed Miss Mee.

'Oh –' she said. 'Well, it's your name, Hild.'

Hild couldn't believe her ears. She'd never won anything before in her life. She grinned a great big grin at Miss Mee, and her green eyes shone.

'Do you know who you're going to give it to?' asked Miss Mee, holding the door open for her.

'Oh, yes, yes,' gasped Hild, making her way out of school with the precious box. Miss Mee watched her staggering across the playground, and shook her head doubtfully.

Next day Hild arrived at school very early. But she didn't burst in as usual and slam the door; she came in very quietly and just stood. Miss Mee turned round to look at her. Hild's golden-orange hair was tied back with a beautiful bow of green satin ribbon.

'Hello, Hild –' began Miss Mee, then stopped, and stared at the ribbon.

'He gave it me,' burst out Hild.

'Gave you what? Who did?' asked Miss Mee.

'The ribbon. My Dad,' said Hild. 'When he opened the basket.'

'But you know it was for someone poor or housebound,' cried Miss Mee.

'He *is* poor,' said Hild. 'He's never got no money.'

'Or someone old,' went on Miss Mee.

'He *is* old – older 'n me, anyway,' said Hild.

'Or someone who's unwell,' said Miss Mee.

'Dad's not well,' said Hild. 'You should see his hand – all swollen up where the cat scratched it.'

Miss Mee stared at Hild angrily. Hild put on her sulky, scowling face and scuffed one foot on the floor.

'Anyway,' she said, 'he's housebound as well today. He's stuck at home with a pain in his tummy.'

'Oh?' said Miss Mee, still very cross. 'What sort of a pain?'

'A greedy pain,' said Hild, scowling. 'Me and Trudi are all right, we weren't greedy. But it serves him right if he's got a pain – he wouldn't let us have no grapes or peaches; he ate them all himself . . .'

The Dinosaurs' Den

Mrs Hubb, the school secretary, came hurrying along the corridor towards Class 1. She put her hand on the classroom door handle, then stopped. There was a large notice stuck on the door. She read it aloud:

'Take a deep breath and count up to ten,
Then come on in to the Dinosaurs' Den.'

'My goodness me,' thought Mrs Hubb. 'That sounds a bit dangerous. But I'll have to go in, Miss Mee is waiting for this sticky tape.'

She went into the classroom and gasped. Hanging from the ceiling were branches and leaves. Stretching all the way along the opposite wall was a long pool of water with plants growing in it and tufts of rushes along its edges. Standing in the water was an enormously long dinosaur. His back and neck touched the ceiling, and he was chewing a mouthful of pondweed.

'He's our diplodocus,' said Barbara.

'And look up in the branches,' said Hild. 'There's some pterodactyls, ready to take off.'

'And look out – on the wall behind you!' said Pete.

Mrs Hubb swung round and gasped again. Coming out from between the tree trunks was a giant creature. It was walking upright, holding its front paws out, ready to grab something to eat. Its jaws were open, and it was baring its pointed teeth.

'That's Tyrannosaurus Rex,' said Wendy. 'I made his claws with foil.'

'Look over here,' said Mary. 'This is a triceratops. I folded the paper to make the frills on his neck – don't you think they're good?'

'And have you seen our fossils?' asked

Ian, pulling Mrs Hubb over to the window-sill. 'Do you see this one? It's coprolite – that's dinosaur dung, turned to stone – honest it is.'

There was so much to see, Mrs Hubb didn't know where to look next.

'My goodness,' she said. 'What a wonderful dinosaurs' den you've made. It's a pity you haven't a real dinosaur; it would feel quite at home in here.'

She gave Miss Mee the sticky tape and went out to ring the hometime bell.

'Now do up your zips and buttons,' said Miss Mee. 'It's bitterly cold outside; it's cold enough for snow.'

Snow did fall in the night; not very deep – just enough to spread a beautiful white cover over roofs, gardens and roads. When Hild woke up, the bedroom was full of brightness. She sat up and peeped round the curtain.

'Snow!' she cried. 'There's snow everywhere – look, Trudi – wake up and look!'

'I've seen snow before,' grunted Trudi, pulling the quilt over her face. She wasn't a bit interested. But Hild was really excited. She loved snow. She loved the beautiful look of it and the cold smell of it; she loved letting snowflakes melt on her tongue or dabbling her fingers in its softness.

She dressed quickly and ran down-stairs; she didn't want to waste a single moment. She pulled on her coat and unbolted the back door. The garden lay smooth and white, like the top of an iced cake. She stepped slowly across the snow. Then she turned and looked behind her; footprints led from the door to where she stood. She bent over to look

at the snow more carefully. Now she could see other footprints, tiny ones, tracks of birds or other little creatures which had been in the garden earlier in the morning. Hild turned round and walked slowly back to the door.

Now she could see another set of tracks, large footprints, which led down the side of the house to the bottles of milk on the doorstep; that must have been the milkman in his wellington boots. Hild wondered what other sorts of footprints there were: she'd like to see what sort of tracks a tiger would make in the snow – or a giraffe – or a kangaroo – or even one of the dinosaurs they'd been talking about at school. She suddenly had an amazing idea.

'Great!' she said giggling to herself. 'I'll play a trick; they'll never guess.'

A few minutes later, after a quick breakfast of a banana and a bag of crisps, she banged the door shut and was on her way up Allotment Lane. She was so early that the footprints she made were the first to mark the fresh snow. She laughed to herself as she pressed her feet down slowly and carefully along the middle of the lane. Soon she turned in through the school gate and stepped across the white playground. She hung her coat up on its peg. Then she put something secret that made her laugh into a carrier bag, and hung that up on her peg too.

Everything was strange and quiet – she realized that she was the first person in school. She tip-toed into Class 1 and sat in the book corner, looking at a book. Then she heard Miss Mee come in and went to talk to her.

'Hello, Hild,' said Miss Mee. 'You beat me to it today.'

'I've been playing a trick,' grinned Hild.

'What sort of a trick?' asked Miss Mee. 'Nice or nasty?'

'Oh, just funny,' said Hild. 'You know our Trudi, don't you?'

'Yes, of course I do,' said Miss Mee, rather surprised at the question.

'Did you know she went snorking last summer?' asked Hild.

'Snorking?' said Miss Mee in a puzzled voice. 'Do you mean snorting, like pigs do?'

'No, snorking,' said Hild. 'Under the

water, with flippers and a sort of tube in her mouth to breathe through, and goggles . . .'

'Oh, *snorkelling*, Hild – you mean snorkelling. Is that what your Trudi did?'

'Yes, snorkelling, that's right,' said Hild. 'Well, I've brought a carrier bag with things in to show you. It's hanging on my peg, it's –'

She didn't finish what she was saying, because the twins burst into the classroom.

'Miss Mee, Miss Mee, we came up the lane, and there's monster tracks, right up the middle of the lane.'

Then Paul and Michael came hurrying in.

'Hey, Miss Mee, we've just come up the lane – we followed some giant footprints and they came across the playground right into school!'

Nasreen and Mary came in next.

'Guess what – there's dinosaur footprints all the way up the lane!'

Soon lots of people were trying to tell

Miss Mee about the dinosaur tracks in the snow. Miss Mee wanted to see them for herself, so the children crowded round her and led her outside – all except Hild. There in the playground, leading from the lane, were huge flat footprints, bigger than those made by any person. They led straight into school.

'Do you think they're brontosaurus footprints?' asked Imdad.

They all stared at the tracks.

'No, they'd be bigger,' said Ian. 'A brontosaurus was as big as fifteen elephants.'

'Perhaps it's a pterodactyl,' said little Larry.

'No, silly, that used to fly – it wouldn't *walk* up the lane, would it?'

'It might be a stegosaurus,' suggested Stevie.

'Or a triceratops,' said Mary.

They stared again at the huge footprints. They were all wondering the same thing.

'Do you think it's a Tyrannosaurus Rex?' whispered Brenda.

Everyone looked round nervously, hoping a Tyrannosaurus Rex wouldn't come lumbering out, looking for fresh meat. Michael said slowly:

'If the footprints go into school and don't come out again, that means he's still in school somewhere.'

They all gasped. A dinosaur wandering round Allotment Lane School! Barbara shivered.

'Let's go back in again, quick,' she said.

They swarmed back into the warm classroom, and shut the door firmly. Hild was there on her own, making a plasticine diplodocus.

'You should have have seen the footprints, Hild,' said Pete excitedly. He moved his hands to show her how huge the footprints were. 'They were long and fat with sort of toe shapes.'

'That wouldn't be toes,' said Hild. 'That'd be claws, sharp claws . . .'

'Did you see a dinosaur go past while we were outside?' asked Larry.

'Well, I might have heard a sort of

roaring noise,' nodded Hild.

Everyone gasped and looked at her.

'And a sort of loud hissing . . .' she went on. 'And a dreadful sort of grunting, like some monster was getting hungry and looking for food . . .'

'Oh!' shrieked everyone, eyes wide with fright. 'Where? Where's it gone? Where is it?'

'Just over there by the coat hooks,' said Hild calmly. 'Shall I show you? – I'm not scared.'

Everyone pressed close to Miss Mee. Little Larry clutched her skirt. Holding their breath, they watched Hild go to her coat hook. She lifted down her carrier bag and turned to look at them all. There was a long silence.

'Where's the dinosaur, then?' whispered Nasreen.

'In this bag,' said Hild.

There was another long silence, while they all stared at her.

'It's the things our Trudi had for snorking,' she explained.

'Snorkelling,' said Miss Mee.

'Yes, that's right,' said Hild.

She opened the bag and took out a snorkel, some goggles – and a huge pair of rubber flippers. She fitted them over her feet to show everyone.

'I wore them up the lane,' she giggled. 'I wanted to see what sort of tracks they'd make. It was a track trick.'

Her fat little cheeks grew bright pink and she giggled again.

'The dinosaur was me,' she said.

Everyone stared at her for several moments. Then suddenly, Paul began to laugh, then Michael, then Asif spluttered with laughter, and the twins and Laura started to giggle too. Soon everybody was laughing at Hild's trick; even Miss Mee's shoulders were shaking.

'Ooh, you rotten meanie, Hild Hooson!' exclaimed Brenda, still giggling. 'You had us all dead scared.'

'But it was a good trick,' said Hild. 'Wasn't it? And I bet they're the best dinosaur tracks you've ever seen – aren't they?

Aren't they?'

And everyone had to nod and laugh and say that they were.

A Chair and a Chain

One winter's day everyone came back cheerfully into the classroom after dinner, with rosy cheeks and sniffing noses – everyone, that is, except Hild. Miss Mee looked round.

'Where's Hild?' she asked.

'In the corridor,' said Asif.

'Her scarf's up on the pipes,' said Mary.

'She said she wouldn't come in,' said Paul. 'I tried to pull her in, but she thumped me.'

At that moment Hild threw open the door and stormed into the room. She flew straight at Paul and pummelled him with her fists.

'That's for throwing my scarf up on the water pipes!' she yelled, then burst into tears. Miss Mee calmed her down and wiped her face.

'You know I can reach your scarf down for you,' she said.

'Yes, but it's not fair,' gulped Hild. 'The boys are always fighting me, and Mrs Doran was cross when I spilt my custard on the dinner table, and then I slipped over on the ice, and then –'

'Oh, poor Hild,' said Miss Mee. 'I think you must have got out of bed on the wrong side this morning.'

'No, I didn't,' said Hild, shaking her head. 'I got out the side I always get out; I can't get out the other side – the wall's there.'

'No, no,' said Miss Mee, 'I meant you've been in trouble all day: everything's been going badly for you today. But –' (she turned to tell everybody) '– now I've got a piece of news for you all. At two o'clock we're going to have a visitor, the Mayor. She's one of the people in charge of our town; she works at the Town Hall, and she's a very important person. She said she'd like to visit

Allotment Lane School, so at two o'clock she'll be coming into this classroom. I expect she'll be wearing her chain-of-office.'

'Like a lavvy chain?' asked Hild. She had cheered up now and was looking interested.

'No,' said Miss Mee. 'This is a chain to show that she's the most important person in the town; she'll be wearing it round her neck.'

'Oh, like we chain our dogs up with?' said Hild.

'Well, no,' said Miss Mee. 'This will be a really pretty chain – more like a necklace – and it'll have a pendant, a sort of picture, hanging from it. Have a good look when she comes in. But now we've got half an hour to tidy up ready for her: can you all help?'

In a moment everyone was scurrying round, putting away bricks and Lego, tidying the tables, putting books back in the bookcase the right way up and throwing bits of rubbish in the bin. Laura decided to tidy the tins of powder paint on the bench. Hild was next to her, bending down brushing spilt sand into a dustpan. Suddenly, one of the tins of powder fell over, and the lid clatterd down onto the floor. Hild leaned forward to pick it up and – whoosh! – a shower of green powder fell over the edge of the bench and down onto Hild's golden-orange head.

'What's that?' asked Hild. She shook her head like a puppy coming out of the water, and a cloud of green powder flew in all directions. She and Laura began to sneeze. Miss Mee turned to look at them.

'Hild!' she exclaimed. She hurried over to the painting bench and ruffled Hild's hair, hard. Most of the powder flew out, but some of it sank down to the roots of her hair, so that the pink skin of her head looked green.

'Merciful heaven!' cried Miss Mee, looking at Hild with a horror. 'Never mind – there's no time to do anything about it now – I'll help to clean you up when the Mayor has gone; she'll be here in five minutes. Now for goodness sake, both of you take a chair and sit in the Quiet Corner with a book until she comes.'

Laura did as Miss Mee said. Hild took a chair too, but not to the Quiet Corner; no, she took it over to the tall cupboard where she knew Miss Mee kept a little mirror on the top shelf. Hild wanted to see what had happened to her hair. She climbed on

to the chair, stood up on tip-toe, stre-e-etching as high as she could and reaching for the mirror. Then – the chair wobbled, her feet slipped, there was a tumble and a crash – and Hild fell down through the space in the back of the chair.

'Ow-oww-ow!' she roared, struggling to stand up. But she couldn't: her fat little bottom was at one side, and her fat little chest was at the other, and she couldn't pull one way or the other.

'I'm stuck!' she yelled. 'I'm stuck, Miss Mee, I'm *stuck*!'

Miss Mee couldn't believe her eyes. She ran to Hild and got hold of her round the waist. She pulled and pulled, but the chair wouldn't shake loose.

'Ian, Nasreen, Imdad!' ordered Miss Mee. 'Pull the chair!'

The three children pulled the chair as hard as they could, and Miss Mee pulled Hild – but they still couldn't get Hild loose.

'It's a bit like a tug-of-war, isn't it, Miss Mee?' asked Ian.

'No, it's not,' screamed Hild.

'Perhaps we'll pull her in two,' said Imdad.

'Don't you dare!' yelled Hild.

At this moment the door opened and the Mayor walked in. She looked at Miss Mee and the children and the chair – and Hild in the middle of it all with a bright red face and greeny-orangey hair – and she knew what to do straightaway.

'Everybody stand back,' she ordered. Everybody moved away from Hild and the chair.

'Now stand on your feet,' she told Hild, 'Stand up straight.'

Hild stood up, with the chair round her waist. The Mayor took hold of the chair and gently pulled it down, wiggling it from side to side as she did it. She looked at Hild's greeny-orangey hair, then at her fat red cheeks streaked with tears.

'What's your name?' she asked, still wiggling the chair. Everyone was watching, not saying a word. Hild looked at the Mayor's smart red hat, and then at the red and gold chain round her neck.

'Hilda Hooson,' she said, in a little voice.

'Oh – I think I know your Dad,' said the Mayor. 'I've met him once or twice at the Town Hall – he's got two dogs, hasn't he?'

'Yes, that's right,' said Hild, grinning with delight. 'Woofer and Barker.'

'Well, then, we're old friends already, you and I, aren't we?' said the Mayor. 'And look – you can step out of the chair now.'

Hild looked down and saw that she wasn't stuck any more; the Mayor had wiggled the chair down Hild's legs and on to the floor. Hild stepped out of the chair, turned it the right way up, and sat on it.

'There, that's better,' said the Mayor. She shook hands with Miss Mee, then sat down on the teacher's chair and looked at everyone.

'I'm going to talk to you for a little while before I look round your classroom,' she said. 'But first I'm going to take my chain off. It's very beautiful – but it's rather heavy. Now where can I put it? – Ah, I know. Perhaps Hilda would look after it for me.'

She leant forward and carefully placed the shining red and gold chain over Hild's head; it rested on her shoulders and hung down over her chest. Hild's eyes shone,

and she sat up very straight. She had never felt so important or so happy before. Now she knew for certain that she hadn't got out of bed on the wrong side.

More Young Puffins

THE GHOST AT NO. 13
Gyles Brandreth

Hamlet Brown's sister, Susan, is just too perfect. Everything she does is praised and Hamlet is in despair – until a ghost comes to stay for a holiday and helps him to find an exciting idea for his school project!

RADIO DETECTIVE
John Escott

A piece of amazing deduction by the Roundbay Radio Detective when Donald, the radio's young presenter, solves a mystery but finds out more than anyone expects.

RAGDOLLY ANNA'S CIRCUS
Jean Kenward

Made only from a morsel of this and a tatter of that, Ragdolly Anna is a very special doll and the six stories in this book are all about her adventures.

SEE YOU AT THE MATCH
Margaret Joy

Six delightful stories about football. Whether spectator, player, winner or loser these short, easy stories for young readers are a must for all football fans.

ONE NIL
Tony Bradman

Dave Brown is mad about football and when he learns that the England squad are to train at the local City ground he thinks up a brilliant plan to overcome his parents' objections and get him to the ground to see them.

ON THE NIGHT WATCH
Hannah Cole

A group of children and their parents occupy their tiny school in an effort to prevent its closure.

FIONA FINDS HER TONGUE
Diana Hendry

At home Fiona is a chatterbox but whenever she goes out she just won't say a word. How she overcomes her shyness and 'finds her tongue' is told in this charming book.

IT'S TOO FRIGHTENING FOR ME!
Shirley Hughes

The eerie old house gives Jim and Arthur the creeps. But somehow they just can't resist poking around it, even when a mysterious white face appears at the window! A deliciously scary story — for brave readers only!

THE CONKER AS HARD AS A DIAMOND
Chris Powling

Last conker season Little Alpesh had lost every single game! But this year it's going to be different and he's going to be Conker Champion of the Universe! The trouble is, only a conker as hard as a diamond will make it possible — and where on earth is he going to find one?